P9-APQ-669

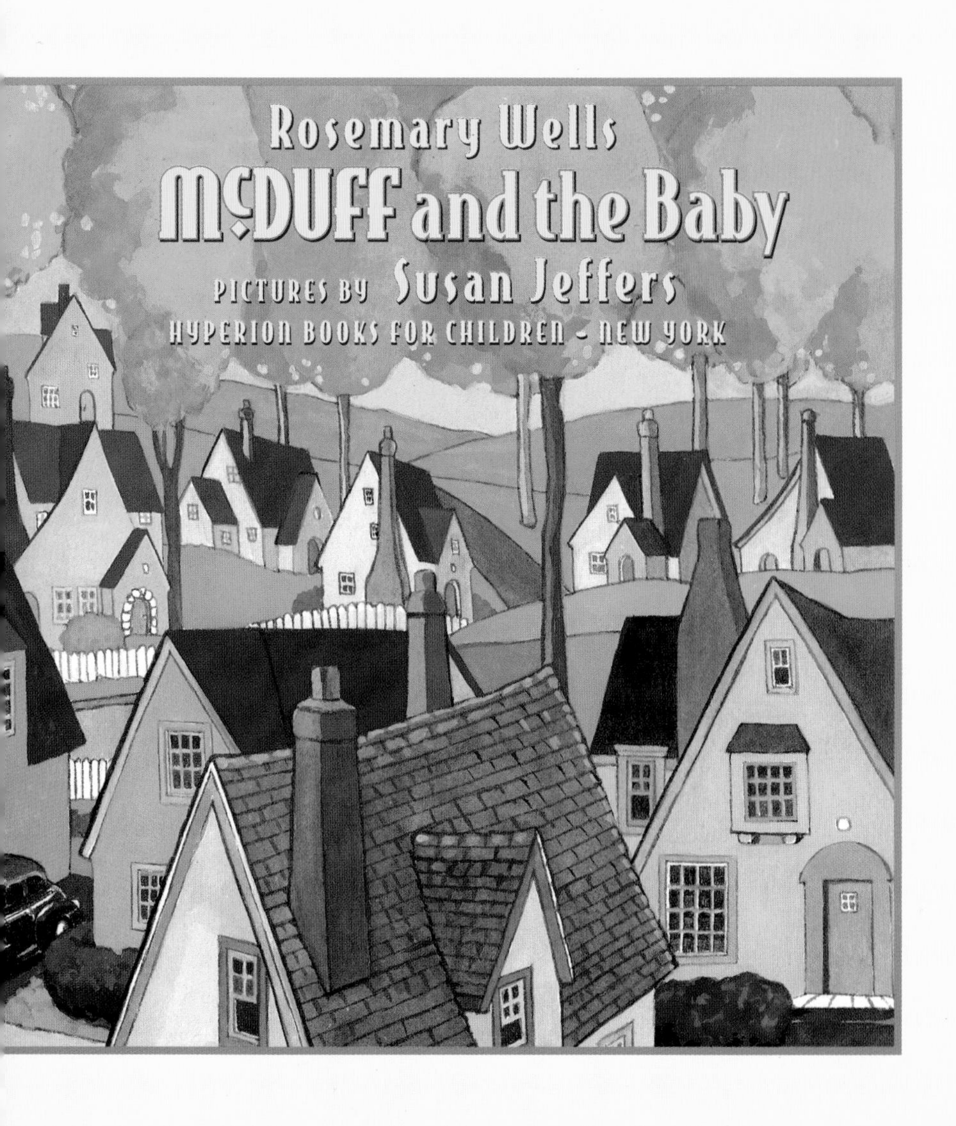
Rosemary Wells
McDUFF and the Baby
PICTURES BY Susan Jeffers
HYPERION BOOKS FOR CHILDREN - NEW YORK

Every night McDuff slept on his very own soft blanket right at the foot of Lucy and Fred's bed.

At breakfast Fred read the comics out loud to McDuff.

In the afternoons Lucy walked McDuff in the woods, where he could smell skunk trails in the leaves.

After supper they all sat on the sofa together and listened to "Music from the Stars" on the radio. Every day in every way McDuff was happy.

But one day a stranger arrived.

It was a baby.

The baby kept Lucy and Fred hopping all day long.

There was no time to read the morning comics out loud.

The carriage would not roll on the woodland path,
so they had to walk on the street.

All the neighbors admired the new baby.

In the evenings the baby interrupted the radio concerts.
She woke everyone up in the middle of the night.

Lucy and Fred hoped McDuff would love the new baby. But the new baby pulled McDuff's beard, and he did not want to be nice.

McDuff growled at the baby from across the room.
The baby just laughed.

McDuff gave the baby terrible squinting looks.
The baby didn't mind at all.

McDuff stopped eating.
“McDuff has stopped eating!” said Lucy.

"I bet he misses the comics," said Fred.

Over cereal and fruit Fred read the newspaper aloud to McDuff.

Then Lucy walked McDuff in the woods. There were hundreds of skunk footprints in the wet leaves.

After supper Lucy and Fred gave McDuff his favorite treat of vanilla rice pudding with sausage slices.

Then they took the radio outside.

In the dark of the garden all four of them sat on lawn chairs and hummed to the "Music from the Stars."

"Woof," said McDuff.
"Woof," said the baby.

First Hyperion Mini edition 2001.

A hardcover edition of *McDuff and the Baby* is available from
Hyperion Books for Children.
 For information address
Hyperion Paperbacks for Children, 114 Fifth Avenue,
New York, New York 10011.
Printed in China